Cinderella's Daughter

Created and Illustrated

By Joan Arlin Hibbs

For Jenna and all true Princesses, children of all ages, and my Prince Charming.

Acknowledgments

Special thanks to:

Robert Walter Hibbs—My constant, patient, love and support;
Joanna DeRungs, Jonelle Kearney—My first youth Consultants;
Sydnie Goodell—Arizona, Second and Third Draft Author's
Editor; Teresa Marcel, Joanna DeRungs, Joan Sexson—Oregon,
Final Proof Author's Editors; Jennifer Hendershot—
Baltimore,MD. Editor

Text Consultants:

Tim Kearney, MA—Teacher, at Palominas, AZ – Market test school;
Leonard J. Marcel, MD—Psychiatrist - Portland, OR; Teresa Marcel,
MA—Counselor - Portland, OR; Kim Hamilton,
LMFT—Psychotherapist (Attachment Disorder Specialist)
McKinleyville, CA; Judith Bigby, MEd—School Consultant,
Astoria, OR

Writing Mentors and support teams:

Walt and Roselyn Morey—Author and spouse, mentors,
supporters, friends and surrogate parents since 1956
Lee and Cicely Roddy—Author and spouse, mentors, teachers and
friends since 1984

Acknowledgment *and* Thank you to:

Donald R. Hamilton—McKinleyville, CA, Master Photographer
for the back cover photograph of the author;
Stephen Ritch—iJoy™ Robotic Massage® Chair, Interactive Health
Inc., for permission to use the iJoy™ chair as the books *Magic* chair.

Pictures
from the
Royal Picture Album

Princess Cinderella and the Crown Prince
The King, Baby Belinda and Fairy Godmother
A Sad Cinderella and Prince
Belinda's Golden Dress
Godmother and Belinda Hovering
Godmother's Cottage
Belinda's Bed
The Magic Mirror
Talking Note
Pantry Door
Melody, Belinda's Kitten
The Stranger, Seth Wilson
Three Table Desks and Chairs
The Teacher of All Teachers
Patsy, Belinda and Juan in the Magic Chairs
Patsy Landing in the Magic Chair
Master Zhao, Godmother, Belinda, Juan,
and Patsy at the Palace

Chapters

Cinderella's Daughter

Once upon a time, Cinderella and the Prince were right in the middle of living *happily ever after*. Then the old King sent a special invitation to the young couple. He asked them to join him for a formal dinner at the main Royal Palace.

"Why do you think the King has invited us to dinner now?" Cinderella asked as she carefully placed the small diamond crown on her head in preparation for an evening with the King.

"Dearest Cinderella, you know my father. He helped me find you by searching throughout the kingdom for my wife-to-be. Remember, he was in such a hurry because he said he longed for grandchildren? He is still constantly reminding us of that," the Prince replied. "Now hurry, you know how upset he gets if we are late."

Sure enough, the King did indeed call the family together to remind Cinderella and his son that he was not getting any younger.

Once again, during dessert—cherry chocolate cake—the King cleared his throat and said, "Well, my children, I am not getting any younger and I do so want to enjoy my grandchildren while I can."

Cinderella smiled and joyfully responded, "My father-in-law, my King, you need not wait any longer."

The Prince chimed in with their wonderful news. "No more waiting, father. Your wish is our wish. We soon will be blessed by the birth of our first child! We were about to visit you to tell you our wonderful news. Then we received your invitation to dinner."

"We are blessed indeed! You have made this old man extremely happy!" exclaimed the happy King.

The Royal Palace sent out a proclamation announcing the anticipated joyful event. The whole kingdom was buzzing with the happy news. As soon as they heard about the expected baby, all the people in the kingdom got right to work preparing for the beloved child of Cinderella and the Prince: the next heir to the throne.

As time for the baby's arrival drew near, all anyone heard was talk about the baby. Would it be a boy or a girl? And would the child become a kind and fair ruler as the King, the Prince and Cinderella were? Even the young children knew their own happiness and comfort were greatly influenced by the nature of the person ruling their tiny kingdom.

At last, the waiting time was complete and the magnificent celebration welcoming a baby girl lasted three days. At the end of the three days, the old King, Cinderella, and the Prince appeared on the palace balcony. The citizens of the kingdom, who had stood in line for many hours, presented their gifts to the new royal child.

Each person had prepared a special gift: the cobbler—tiny pink leather shoes; the baker—pink cakes; and the florist brought an armload of miniature pink roses. Held snugly in her happy grandfather's arms, the new little Princess was introduced to her subjects. The crowd pressed forward to get a better look.

"Look at her shiny penny-colored hair!" someone exclaimed.

"Surely our little Princess is the most beautiful baby ever born!" one woman, with four children of her own, exclaimed. The crowd cheered in agreement.

"What's her name to be?" the baker shouted out.

Just then there was a flutter and a twinkling of lights, and Cinderella's fairy godmother appeared on the balcony.

The King handed his little granddaughter to her. "Please name her, Fairy Godmother," he said. "You know how important it is to give just the right name to a child."
The fairy godmother looked deeply into the baby's clear blue green eyes and held up a hand for silence. It became so quiet you could hear a mouse squeak.
"Her name shall be Belinda, which means beautiful. She shall also have another name. I will reveal her second name when the time is correct. Now, I present to you, Belinda." Godmother held Belinda up high so everyone could see her. With the naming done, the godmother returned the baby to her grandfather and thanked him for the honor of naming her newest godchild. Then she tenderly kissed all four royal family members farewell, and disappeared as quickly as she had appeared, in a swirl of twinkling lights.
The people of the land were very proud and happy to have such a lovely little Princess. Everyone sang and worked as happiness spread throughout the Kingdom.
Cinderella and the Prince spent most of their days playing with and enjoying their new baby. Belinda was a cheerful and healthy child; she rarely cried. Her every need was attended to even before she had a chance to cry. Servants in the palace all volunteered to help care for her or play with her, and took turns carrying the baby Belinda everywhere. Belinda was never alone and never sad. And with each passing day, she grew more and more beautiful.

Princess Belinda

Time passed happily until one day Cinderella and the Prince were watching their daughter play with some of the palace servants, and they realized something was not quite as it should be. They were disturbed by what they saw.

"Darling," Cinderella said, "look, Belinda is nearly three years old now and she has never taken a step. She is carried everywhere."

"Yes," the Prince said, "she is so lovely that everyone wants to touch her and be near her. They do everything for her. She does nothing for herself. I am not sure that is really healthy for her development."

As her parents watched, they began to pay closer attention and noticed that Belinda was *ordering* people to do this and that. The servants did exactly as she commanded. At the early age of three, Belinda knew she had power over anyone she met. She did not ask for anything; she demanded or ordered it. Worse yet, she did not ever say "please" or "thank you!"

Cinderella and the Prince's feeling of unease grew stronger. However, citizens of the kingdom were happy, and so charmed by Belinda's beauty, that the royal couple decided to do nothing about their uneasiness.

Several more years passed before that first sense of uneasiness developed into full alarm. All was definitely *not* well with the little Princess. By the time Belinda was six years old, she had developed into a moody girl. She pouted for hours when she was told she would have to walk and feed herself. She would take only a few steps and then throw herself on the floor screaming and crying while pulling at her long, silken hair.

When servants brought her favorite food and did not feed it to her, she would throw the food at anyone in the room, even her mother and father.

With each passing day, Cinderella and the Prince were more and more concerned that their beautiful daughter was becoming a mean, thoughtless, little girl. She definitely was not behaving like a true Princess!

Late one evening, just before Belinda's seventh birthday, Cinderella sat on the balcony of the palace staring at the stars in the sky. Tears were sliding down her cheeks.

The Prince joined her and put his comforting arms around her. "Whatever is it that makes you so sad, my love?" the Prince asked.

Cinderella cried, "Oh, my dear husband! Our little Princess has become such an unpleasant child. She treats everyone exactly the way my own stepsisters treated me! I cannot allow it, but I don't know what to do."

The Prince paced and thought, and paced some more. "I've seen it too, dear. Belinda demands only the best of everything for herself. Although she has plenty, she will not share anything. Just this evening she took toys away from two of the servant's children."

Cinderella felt certain that her heart would break. "This will never do! We cannot allow our daughter to be so cruel. Have you noticed, she does not have any friends? Even children of the other royal families will no longer play with her. What can we do to help our daughter?"

The once happy couple talked and thought. Even after they went to bed they talked some more, but did not come up with a good plan about how to help Belinda. It was close to midnight when Cinderella had an inspiration. She sat up in bed and said, "let's ask my fairy godmother! She'll know exactly what we should do."

"Good idea!" said the Prince. "Let's try to sleep now. I'm sure your godmother can help us work out what to do about Belinda's behavior. We shall contact her first thing in the morning."

They slept fairly well, believing that they would soon have a solution to their problem.

Morning found Belinda screaming at her chambermaid even before her parents were awake. "You stupid, stupid girl! I never, never get out of bed before I have my tea. Bring it now. And I want strawberries with my cereal. Be sure they are ripe and plump." Belinda sat in bed with her arms folded across her chest and made a fierce face. "Do it, now!"

"But Princess," the maid whispered cautiously, "it is winter and there are no ripe strawberries this time of year. I cannot—"

Belinda screamed and threw a vase at the maid's head. "Never say 'cannot' to me! You stupid, ugly girl! You will be fired if you don't find strawberries for me at once! Now go, get out of my sight!"

The girl ducked, so the vase only brushed the top of her head." Yes, Princess! As you wish, Princess." She darted down the hall crying, "Whatever can I do? Oh dear, oh dear! There are no strawberries anywhere in the kingdom. I'm finished, I'm through!"

Cinderella and the Prince rushed into their daughter's room. "Belinda, what is all this ruckus? Why was your maid crying?" her parents asked.

"I want strawberries. *Now!* That stupid girl said there are none to be found." The little Princess slapped her hand hard on the pillow beside her and made her most horrible scowling face. "If I don't get strawberries, I shall hold my breath until I faint and then you'll be sorry."

With that, Belinda took in a deep breath and held it as her parents helplessly looked on.

"There are no strawberries this time of year, my darling,"

Cinderella said as she sat beside her daughter trying to smooth her hair and calm her. The Princess simply pushed her mother's hands away and continued to hold her breath.

"Belinda," her father said in his most serious voice," you must breathe at once. Stop this! You are turning blue!"

"I have strawberries for the child," someone said from the window-seat. "Here you are, my darling. Fairy Godmother floated over to the bedside of the little Princess. She carried a lovely, silver serving tray piled high with strawberries and whipped cream. "Did you not hear her? My little goddaughter wants strawberries."

Cinderella and the Prince's mouths fell open as Belinda began to eat the strawberries with both hands. She was finishing the last berry and wiping the cream from her chin when the fairy godmother signaled Cinderella and the Prince to follow her out into the hallway. They followed her quietly until they were out of Belinda's earshot.

"I am amazed at you, Godmother," Cinderella protested. "If you have come to help, why did you give Belinda the strawberries when she is acting so dreadful?"

"Don't worry. It is just a little bit of magic to help you see how unmanageable your daughter has become and just how far one must go to gain her cooperation. For now, it is a way to get her to pay attention to *me*," said Fairy Godmother as she touched the side of her head and winked at Belinda's startled parents. "You were going to summon me, weren't you? Well, do you want to hear my wonderful ideas?" Cinderella and the Prince mutely nodded.

"You have finally noticed my little goddaughter is far from being the perfect Princess." Both parents nodded again. "Do you know why she behaves as she does? Why she is such an unpleasant child?"

"Honestly, I do not know what has caused her to become just like my unkind stepsisters. Why is Belinda such a cruel child?" Cinderella dried her eyes.

Cinderella's fairy godmother twirled her wand in one hand. She smiled as she did an excited little dance. "Belinda is being so cruel and selfish because she has never felt loneliness or sorrow or wanted for anything. She is only concerned with herself. She believes she is better than anyone else just because she is beautiful and a princess. And everyone reinforces that false idea by catering to her demands or giving in to her tantrums. So now, her heart is untouched by love and has not grown since she was born."

Cinderella and the Prince looked puzzled. "Her heart? You mean she does not love anyone but herself?" the Prince asked. "Right you are, my dear." Godmother went out on the balcony and sat on a lounge chair. The royal couple followed her and pulled their chairs up close to listen carefully to Godmother. "Belinda," the eager fairy godmother pointed at the bedroom where the Princess was being dressed, "does not know what loves, so she has no loving heart. Now, it is very, very necessary to have a loving, considerate heart—especially if one is to be loved, and most certainly if one is to rule a kingdom some day." "Right! That is absolutely, positively true," Cinderella said. "My stepsisters did not have loving or considerate hearts.

"What do you think we should do? Shall we send her to a boarding school? Will that help?" the worried Prince pleaded." We truly need your help, and quickly!"

"Oh, I've got it. Yes, I definitely have a perfect plan." The fairy godmother twirled excitedly in circles sending sparkles flying in all directions. Then she stood quite still and pointed her wand at Cinderella. "Just let her come visit me for a while. I will school her carefully in the ways of a Princess."

Cinderella's face went pale. "Let her go visit with you? Why? How could we do that? We love her." Just then, Belinda joined them on the balcony.

"Mother, when are you going to get me some clothes made of spun gold? These silly cloth things are fine for you and Daddy, but I want beautiful dresses and shoes made of spun gold to match my golden hair."

"Belinda," her father scolded, "this is not a wealthy kingdom and we do not need clothes made of gold; that would be very wasteful. We as rulers are responsible for feeding and looking after the poor in our kingdom. We take care of orphans and widows. There simply is not enough in our treasury to pay for the expensive clothes for which you ask."

"Then you just get it, Daddy. Stop giving those silly, poor people our money. Let them starve, for all I care." Belinda stamped her tiny foot and looked at her fairy godmother. "You can get me golden clothes, can't you?" she asked smiling her best charming smile.

Godmother danced around Belinda. "Yes, my dear. Yes I can, I can!" she chanted.

The Prince had heard enough. "No! You shall not have golden clothes and you shall not have even one more strawberry. Belinda, it's time for you to go to your tutor and get your lessons about your royal duties."

Belinda placed her hands firmly on her hips and said, "I don't have to! I will do just what I want, and there is nothing you or anybody else can do about it. I will find someone who will give me the things I want. You two are mean, and ugly, and hateful, and I hope I never see you again!" With that, the little Princess stomped into the palace shouting at everyone in sight. "Send for the tailor, I am ordering new clothes!" Cinderella moaned, the Prince paced and rubbed his head, and the fairy godmother stood patiently twirling her wand.

Suddenly the Prince stopped pacing. "What did you mean when you said we should allow Belinda to stay with you for lessons?"

"We love her dearly, Fairy Godmother. Parting with her is not easy to consider. If it will help her …" Cinderella fell silent and then asked, "How long would you want her to visit? Could we see her once in a while?"

"I will not keep her for long. My lessons happen quickly. It will seem to Belinda that she is with me a long time, but in reality, it will be only a short while. You know that I can take good care of her. I promise to teach her the special lessons of the heart. So, what do you think? Will you let her come with me? You may think it over."

The Prince took Cinderella over to a corner table where they talked quietly. Finally, they walked to where the godmother was waiting patiently. They agreed to let Godmother take charge of their little daughter, "but only if she will agree to go with you. She must *want* to go," her parents said.

Godmother's disappearing lights began swirling as she chuckled happily and said gently, "You just leave everything at home. I will be back in a flash. Kindly bring Belinda to the balcony at once." The godmother disappeared, and Cinderella and the Prince went to find Belinda.

In about two twinkles of a star, the fairy godmother reappeared on the balcony with a wonderful, golden dress and golden slippers.

Belinda, Cinderella, and the Prince were just walking through the doorway onto the balcony and Belinda was screaming, "No! No!" as she twisted away from the strong grip her father had other hand. "I don't have to go with you! I won't do anything you tell me to do. Leave me alone!" Then the little Princess spied the golden dress and slippers in Fairy Godmother's hands. She pulled away from her father and ran to embrace the spun gold dress.

"Is this what you wanted?" her fairy godmother asked.

"Oh, yes! This is exactly what I wanted. Let me have them! I will get my maid to help me put them on." Belinda tugged at the dress and shoes held tightly in fairy godmother's hands.

"First, Belinda," her godmother said, "I want to know, will you come live with me for a while? I would greatly enjoy your company. This dress and slippers are yours if you agree to stay with me."

"Of course! I would rather stay with you any old day. Mother and Daddy are really becoming boring and mean. You can give me everything I need, right?" Belinda asked.

"Right you are, my child." Godmother released the dress and slippers, and Belinda ran inside to change. "I will provide everything you *need.* She winked at Cinderella. *"*She agrees! I will come for her tonight at exactly midnight. Have her things ready. A promise is a promise." Before anyone could speak, twinkling lights appeared and she was gone.

Belinda pranced out onto the balcony in her golden dress and slippers. "Where is my fairy godmother? I want to show her how beautiful I look. I want to go home with her."

Cinderella and the Prince brushed away traces of tears and hugged their little daughter.

Then the Prince said, "Fairy Godmother will return tonight at midnight. We have the rest of the day to have a party and let your people come say goodbye to you. Then we will gather your favorite things for you to take on your trip."

Belinda looked surprised. "But Father, I won't need anything. My fairy godmother will give me everything I need. You can be sure it will be a lot nicer than anything you have ever given me. Let's have the party. I want everybody to see how beautiful I am in my new golden clothes."

The entire kingdom came to the party for Belinda. Many of the people were *not* sad to hear she was going away to visit her godmother, for she had treated them badly and hurt many feelings. Although Belinda was the most beautiful person in the Kingdom, she was also the least liked.

At the final stroke of midnight, the fairy godmother appeared on the balcony outside of Belinda's bedroom. Cinderella, the Prince, and Belinda were there to greet her.

"Well, well, don't you look lovely?" Godmother said to Belinda." Where are your things? We must leave at once."

Belinda danced about in her tiny, golden slippers. "This is all I am taking. I know you will give me everything I need, and it will be much better than anything Mother and Daddy have. I am ready to leave this stupid old castle."

"All right then, please kiss and hug your mother and father good bye," her godmother said. "We will be gone in a flash. Oh dear Cinderella, no need to be so sad," Fairy Godmother continued, as she handed a large silver mirror to Cinderella. "I will leave you this looking glass. Each morning at dawn look into it and you will be able to see your child and know that she is well. She will have one just like it in her bedroom at my cottage."

"Thank you, Fairy Godmother. You do understand that it is so hard to let our child go from our sight. Please, take good care of her and bring her back soon," Cinderella pleaded.

"Don't worry about your child. You can trust me. The next time you see her will be tomorrow morning in the mirror. She can see you too if she wishes. The mirror has a two-way switch activated by a loving desire of the heart."

The Prince kissed and hugged his little daughter and looked into her eyes. "When you are home again, I believe you will truly be better prepared to take on your role of little Princess. Go with your fairy godmother. Now remember, we love you."

As soon as they had said their farewells, Godmother told Belinda to hold onto her tightly and then lifted her up onto her back. She waved her magic wand and said, "Belinda will be back in a short time, if all goes as planned." The two disappeared in a burst of light.

The Prince and Cinderella held each other and gazed up into the night sky watching their trail of light. "She will be fine," the Prince said. Cinderella nodded and looked at the magic mirror. "Belinda's lessons begin tomorrow," the Prince continued. "We will be able to see her each morning in that looking glass, so let's trust Fairy Godmother."

"Yes," Cinderella replied, "I know she must learn to be considerate of others and most importantly, Belinda will be safe. But I shall miss her."

As they turned to go into the castle, Cinderella and the Prince heard sounds of Belinda's tinkling laughter. They smiled at each other and went to bed sure their little daughter was in the protective care of the amazing Fairy Godmother.

Belinda's Lessons Begin

Sit on this pillow." A large, soft pillow magically appeared in the middle of the floor. "*Think* of each object you want in your room and where you want it. It will materialize as soon as you can picture every detail of it. You may furnish your room as you choose." Belinda sat down on the pillow, looked at the stone floor, and tried to think. "I can't think of things, Godmother. Everything was always in my room at home since I was a baby. Can't I just have the same things I had at home?"

"Yes, if that is what you truly want." Godmother waved her magic wand and smiled. "Just remember, you must choose tonight how you will furnish your room. No changes allowed. But *you must* picture each object in your mind. I cannot do it for you."

Because Belinda was used to just ordering whatever she wanted, she said, "Give me everything in this room exactly the same as it was at home."

"Oh, no," Godmother said shaking her head, "*you* must think of each object exactly as you want it. Sit quietly and picture every corner of your bedroom at the palace. Some effort on your part is required since this is to be your room. Each object will appear as you *clearly* picture it in your mind. You had better start now or you won't have a bed to sleep in. It is way past your usual bedtime."

Belinda sat in the center of the room and closed her eyes. She was feeling very sleepy. Finally, she remembered her big bed with the tall posts and white, lace curtains over and around it. She thought of the puffy satin quilt, the feather mattress, the four feather pillows, and the ever-so-soft, brushed cotton sheets printed with tiny pink rosebuds. As she pictured the bed, it appeared right under her.

Belinda gave a great sigh, lay back in the soft, warm covers, and snuggled her head into the pillows.

Before she could think up another thing for her room, she was fast asleep.

Godmother stood on her tiptoes and kissed Belinda on the forehead. "Sleep well, my little Princess. Tomorrow we set in motion the rest of your lessons. This was just a little test of focusing your mind power. Too bad, you only managed to think up this bed. Oh well, at least you have a very cozy place to sleep. That's actually all you will need to begin your adventures here." Godmother yawned, turned around twice, and was instantly in her own bed upstairs. "I am a bit tired myself," she said." Tomorrow is a big day." She fell asleep with a smile of contentment on her lips.

Alone

Belinda awakened to birds singing outside her bedroom window. For a moment, she did not know exactly where she was. The bed she was in was hers, of course. She sat up, rubbed her eyes, and looked around. And then she remembered: she was in her fairy godmother's little cottage far into the woods.

"Fairy Godmother," she called, "where are you? I am very hungry." She hopped out of bed, then stood still and slowly turned around, carefully surveying the whole room. "Fairy Godmother, come out. Where are my things? There is nothing in this room but my bed."

"Don't you remember?" Her fairy godmother's voice rang out from far above her, "You fell asleep before thinking up anything other than your bed."

"Godmother!" Belinda cried at the top of her lungs, "where are you? I cannot see you. Come out at once! This is not the least bit funny! I want my breakfast!"

"Oh, I'm much too busy today for breakfast," Godmother replied, as she suddenly appeared sitting on the foot of Belinda's bed. "You will find your breakfast in the kitchen. I am on my way to a fairy godmother's meeting."

"What?" screeched Belinda. "You are leaving me? I don't know anything about your stupid house. How can I manage alone? You better just cancel your old meeting."

"Oh I *must* attend this meeting. Now listen carefully. You are quite safe here. I am leaving you with some of my favorite magical friends. You will be fine."

"What magical friends?" Belinda whined. "Are they your servants?"

"No, not servants. These special friends are not people, so anticipate some fun surprises. Each helper will appear as you need them. No introductions will be required; you will know at once that they are *my* friends. I should not be away very long. And you know I will return in a twinkling if you really need me. Now, go to the kitchen and have your breakfast and enjoy the day." With that she disappeared again, as always, in a whirl of the twinkling lights.

Belinda made a quick search of her room but found no trace of her godmother. She saw nothing familiar but her bed. And since she did not find any other clothes either, she decided to wear her wonderful golden dress and shoes.

Her stomach made a hungry, rumbling noise. "Well, where is that kitchen?" she asked aloud, and ran out the pink door and right into the cozy, little living room. There she found only a soft, wool blanket on a small couch facing the stone fireplace, and two large wing chairs near a window. A few knickknacks and a lamp with a flowered shade sat on a wooden table between the chairs. "Nothing here for me to eat," she said, and ran to the end of the hallway where she found the kitchen.

In the kitchen was a large round table with a blue and white checkered cloth. On top of the cloth was a beautiful tray with a bowl of strawberries, milk and sugar, a glass of apple juice, and two fluffy, hot biscuits with butter melting on top. Belinda rushed to the food and grabbed berries in both hands. She gobbled them down as fast as she could push them into her mouth. Reaching for the biscuits, she noticed her hands were red from the berry juice and wiped them on the front of her dress. After finishing every crumb of food, she sat back in one of the wooden, high-backed chairs and glanced around the kitchen.

The kitchen was small and had only the table and one other wooden chair, a white cooking stove, and a white sink with a window above it. There was a towel hanger on the wall draped with dish drying towels. Also on the towel hanger was a bright blue apron. Belinda reached for a slip of paper peeking out of the apron pocket. She could see her name on it. Her name was printed on all of her things at the palace so she thought the note might be for her.

"I wonder what it says," Belinda said. "Maybe I should learn to read." The note contained several lines of writing but she could not read it. "Oh well, Princesses do not need to read. It's just too much work. Besides, I can always get someone to read for me." She made a face at the note, crumpled it up and threw it into the corner.

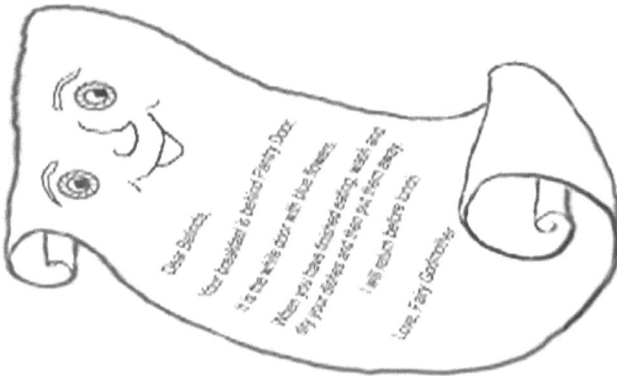

Then something amazing happened—the note talked! "That hurt! I am a message from your godmother. You had better find out what I say. It might be important."
Quickly she picked up the note and smoothed it out on the table.

"Thank you. Can you read what my message says?" asked the voice of the note.

"Of course not, you silly thing. I'm a princess. I don't have to know how to read. Just tell me what your message says."

"Well, I am not certain I *should* tell you. You are quite impolite for a real princess. Are you sure you are an honest to goodness princess?"

Belinda reached for the note. "Tell me the message or I will crumple you up again. What is your message?"

"Oh, very well. My message says, 'Dear Belinda, after you have breakfast please wash and dry your dishes and place them in the cupboard to the left of the sink. If I am not back by lunch, you can find everything you need behind the white pantry door. Be sure to do these few chores before you have lunch.'"

Belinda looked at the wall to her right and saw a white door with little blue flowers painted on it. "'And be sure to make your bed. Love, Fairy Godmother.' End of message," said the Note.

Belinda grabbed the note and squashed it in her fist. "See here, I will not do servants' work! Do you hear, Godmother? This is what I think of your message." She threw the wadded note into the stove. "I will do as I please," declared Belinda. "After all, I *am* a princess! I'll just stay in bed until Godmother comes back." She stomped off to her bedroom. To her surprise, the pink door to her room now had a large, silver mirror hanging on it. For a moment she did not know it was her own image facing her.

"Who are you?" Belinda demanded, a little tremble in her voice. "Why are you so dirty? And … Oh," she cried. "It's me! But it can't be! My beautiful golden hair is a mess and my lovely golden dress is all berry-stained. I look just awful!"

Back to the kitchen she ran. At the sink, she washed her hands and then rubbed at the stains on her dress with one of the dishtowels. But no matter how hard she rubbed, the berry stains would not come out. Rushing back to the mirror, she looked at herself and tried to comb her hair by running her fingers through it. She only made it look worse. "Oh, dear!" she began to cry, I'm not beautiful anymore, and this dress is horrible. I hate it!" She tore at the golden dress until she stood before the mirror in her white, cotton under dress. "I must find something to wear." Then she remembered her godmother's blue apron.

The Magic Mirror Back in the kitchen, she took the apron from the rack and wrapped it around herself. The apron was far too large for Belinda, but it was clean. "Now," she said, "I am just going to sit in bed and wait for Fairy Godmother to come back and take care of me."

For a long while, Belinda watched the birds and two squirrels playing in the trees outside, but they eventually scampered away. Then she stared at the ceiling and then at the stones in the floor. When she grew tired of that, she stared at the plain, undecorated walls until she was so tired of waiting she screamed, I'm bored! I'm hungry!" There was no response to her outburst.

She lay quietly until she remembered what the note had said. She jumped out of bed and headed for the white door in the kitchen. The door had no handle. There seemed to be no way to open it. She pushed on it, then she pounded on it, then she gave it a kick and shouted, "Open up, you stupid door!"

"I am not stupid, young lady," a voice said.

Belinda jumped back and asked in a tiny voice, "Is that you, door? Can you talk too?"

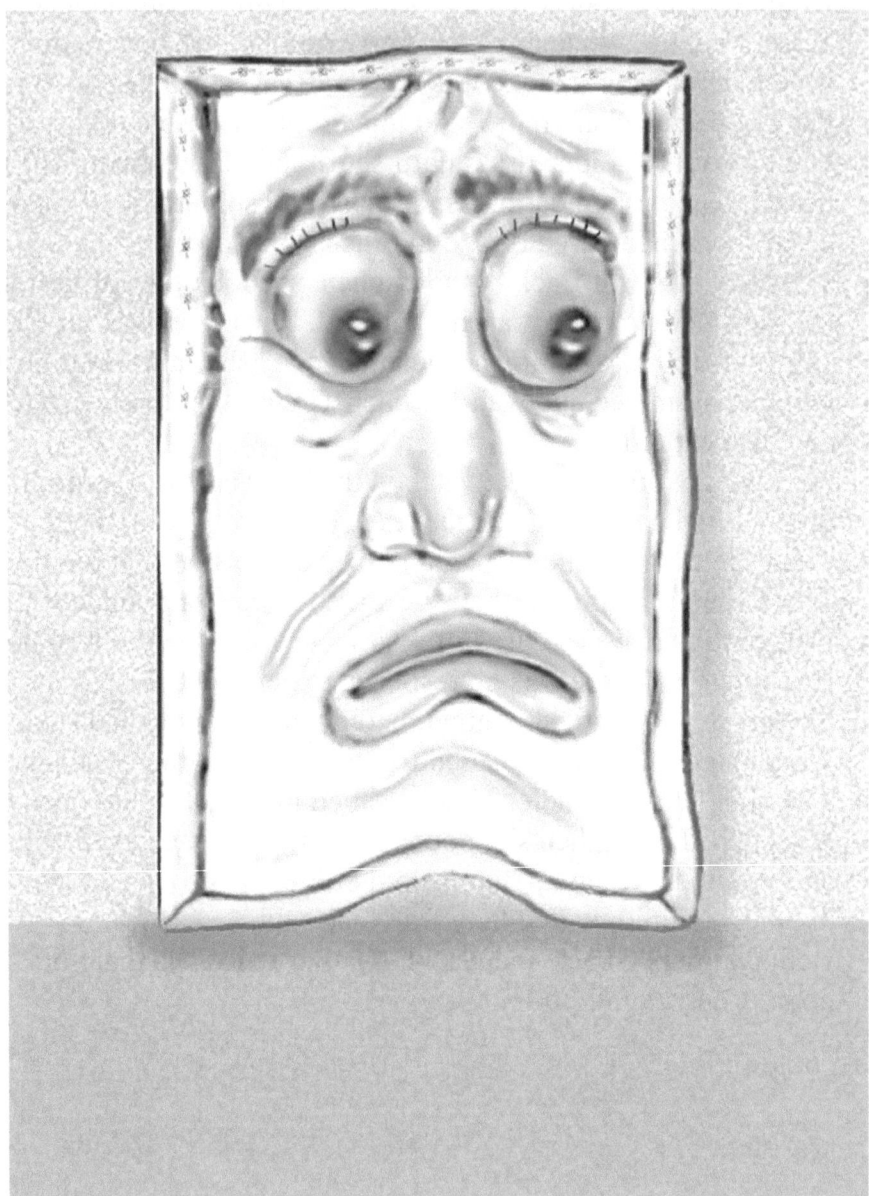

"Indeed I can talk. My name is Pantry Door and I think you need to learn a few manners. At least some common courtesy is required. Even I know that."

"My godmother said I could find my lunch behind you. You just better open up or else," Belinda said, and she gave the door another kick.

"Or else, what?" the door replied. "You can't hurt me. Have you done anything the note told you to do? And besides, you have not once said, 'please.'"

"Why should I? And what does 'please' mean anyway?" Belinda asked.

"*Please*, dear girl, is a short form for, 'if it pleases you to do so.' Or, another way to say it is, 'if it makes you *happy* to do so then do this for me.' And right now it does *not please* me to do anything for a thoughtless child who will not clean her own dirty dishes or make her own bed."

"I won't, I won't!" Belinda stomped her foot. "I'll scream and cry until you open and give me something to eat. The white pantry door did nothing, so Belinda began to scream at the top of her lungs and then she rolled around on the floor crying even louder.

Nothing happened, and not a sound could be heard in response to her continued screaming and crying. The door was silent. It now seemed merely a door with no voice.

Eventually Belinda became tired out by her loud screaming and crying. Completely exhausted, she lay on the floor looking up at the table with the tray of dirty dishes. "Oh, all right, I'll clean the dishes. But I don't really know how. I'll just wash them the way I wash my hands."

She took the tray over to the sink and ran warm water over each dish. Then she got a towel, dried the dishes, and placed them in a nearby cupboard. With her hands on her hips, she turned to the door and said, "Now, open up." There was only silence.

"Open up, Pantry Door," Belinda demanded. "I cleaned my dishes."

From inside the stove she heard a little voice, "There's more." Belinda peaked into the stove and saw the crumpled note she had so angrily thrown in there. "More what?" she asked.

"More chores. Make your bed," the note reminded her.

"My bed? I'm supposed to make my own bed? Never!" Belinda scoffed. "A princess does not do any of this. What do you think servants are for?"

Silence met her question and silence continued until a very hungry Belinda said, "All right, I'll see if I can make my bed." She walked very slowly to her bedroom.

The bed was as she had left it, a jumbled mess. Belinda puffed the pillows and pulled the fluffy white cover over them just as she had seen the servants do. "That's good enough." She folded her arms across her chest and studied her bed. It did not look at all like the freshly made beds at the palace. There were lumps and wrinkles everywhere, but it was a *bit* better.

Back to the kitchen she ran. "Open up, you silly old door," she cried. "I am really hungry now."

"Sorry, I cannot open for you," the door said.

"Whatever is it now?" Belinda wondered. "I washed my dishes and I made my bed. Oh, I know, *please* open, Door."

As soon as Belinda uttered *"please,"* the door opened wide. Belinda looked through the doorway and all she saw was a single slice of bread and a small glass of milk sitting on the shelf.

"Is this all you have for me?" Belinda whined.

"Well, it is not my best," Pantry Door said. "But it is all I wanted to do for you. You really didn't finish your work, You know. You put the dishes in the wrong cupboard and your bed still looks unmade."

"I don't care. I'm hungry." She grabbed the bread and gobbled it down and drank the milk in three huge gulps. She did not notice that the door had closed behind her and she was shut inside the empty pantry.

Turning to leave, Belinda saw the door was now closed. "Let me out, you stupid door!" She shouted and pounded her fists on the door.

Again there was only silence. "Please let me out, Door," she said in a nearly sweet voice.

Nothing happened. "I said 'please'. What now?" "What about, 'thank you?'" asked the door.

"Why?" Belinda asked. "I worked hard for my food. What does 'thank you' mean anyway?"

"The little bit of work you did was just cleaning up after yourself. It was *your* breakfast dishes and *your* bed," the door replied. "And a real princess would know what 'thank you' means."

"Of course I know," Belinda said. "princesses are not required to say such things. Only dumb servants and my subjects must say your silly old 'please' and 'thank you.'"

The door moaned and squeaked, but remained shut.

Belinda swallowed hard three times and said, "Oh phooey! *Thank you* for the bread and milk. Now, *please*, let me out."

Ever so slowly, the door groaned open. Belinda walked into the kitchen and the door slammed shut behind her. "I hate this place!" Belinda screamed at the top of her lungs. "I want to go home!"

"Dear, dear, you can't do that. A promise is a promise." It was her fairy godmother's voice.

Belinda searched the kitchen for her. "Where are you?" She peeked into every cupboard. "Stop hiding from me," she demanded as she peeked under the dishtowels. "I want to go home! Now! You made me come here. Now take me back home!" she cried, standing in the middle of the room shaking her tight little fists at the air.

"Oh, I didn't make you come here." Godmother materialized sitting on the wooden chair by the table. "Oh, no, I didn't *make* you come here. I could never make you do anything. No, no, I would never force you to do things," she chuckled. "Yes, you did. You took me away from my mother and father. Take me back home!" Belinda shouted and stamped her foot.

Fairy Godmother went to the mirror on the pink door and motioned Belinda to follow her. "Here, let us see what truly happened, Belinda. Take a look back at the day we left the palace."

They looked into the mirror. There in the mirror was the castle scene of the day Belinda had wanted strawberries and none could be found.

"Why, that's me at the palace," Belinda said. "See, I'm all clean and beautiful. I want to go home. I want to be beautiful again."

"Keep watching and listening, Belinda. This is the part when you put on the golden dress. Listen carefully," Godmother said and pointed her magic wand at the mirror. Belinda saw herself dancing in her golden dress and agreeing to go with her godmother, and she heard herself say she no longer wanted to live with her parents.

"Well, you tricked me. You gave me what I wanted then but now you won't. You said you would give me everything I wanted."

"Oh, Oh, listen just a bit more. I said I would provide everything you *need* not everything you *want*. We have all we need right here. Now quiet down. You will go home when you have become more like a little princess, not before. You have many lessons ahead of you before you are a *true* princess," Fairy Godmother said sweetly. "A bargain is a bargain."

Belinda shook her head. "My mother will come and get me. Wait and see. She will see how awful I look, and you will be sorry you are so mean to me."

"Your mother looked in on you this morning before you were even awake. In her magic mirror she saw you asleep in your bed, safe and happy. But, come along, Belinda. You truly are a sight. Let's get you clean and in some proper clothes."

Fairy Godmother took her hand and led Belinda to another room where a huge bathtub full of warm water and mounds of bubbles awaited her.

"Please, get into the tub, Belinda," Godmother said. "You will feel much better after you have had a bath." Godmother helped her undress and get into the tub. "Now, while you soak clean, let's have a little talk about today."

Belinda frowned. "It was the worst day of my entire life. Nothing was fun! I had to work hard. I had to do things for myself. I even got shut in the pantry by that mean, old door."

Godmother smiled. "I am sorry you were so unhappy. But tell me, Belinda, did you learn anything useful today?"

"I learned I don't like being ugly and dirty! I hate not having servants." Belinda settled back in the warm water and thought she liked it when the bubbles tickled her nose. She realized she had never enjoyed a bath so much in her entire life. She felt strangely relaxed and happy.

Godmother brought a fluffy pink towel and helped her dry off as she stepped out of the tub. Once she was dry, Belinda said, "What shall I wear? My golden dress is ruined."

"I have a simple cotton dress for you," Godmother said. "And here is a small apron, just like mine. You will find these clothes much more useful living here in the forest and when doing house chores. Here are some nice, sturdy, leather shoes."

Belinda opened her mouth to protest the plain clothes, but stopped. She ran to the mirror on her door. "Let me see how I look." To her surprise, she noticed she looked beautiful, even in the ordinary clothes.

Fairy Godmother walked over and stood behind Belinda, placing her hands on her shoulders. "What else did you learn today, my child?"

"I learned—" Belinda looked into the shining eyes of her fairy godmother. "I learned that asking nicely got me the things I wanted much faster than if I ask in a mean way. Actually, it was the *only* way I could get *anything*."

Then a fantastic thing happened. Belinda said, "thank you, Godmother, for the nice bath and the clothes. I do feel better when I am clean."

The light from Godmother's smile could be seen all the way to the castle where Cinderella and the Prince lived. "You are very welcome, Belinda," Godmother replied. "Now, let's get to a few more chores before we ask Pantry Door for our supper. And tomorrow, we'll clean the fireplace. It was one of your mother's favorite jobs when she was a very young girl, because everyone left her there in peace and quiet. Did you know, sitting among fireplace cinders and daydreaming got her the name Cinderella? Cinderella means little one of the ashes."

Belinda shook her golden curls. "I didn't know that. Did you know my mother when she was my age? Tell me more about my mother, please. How did she become a true princess?"

"That, my dear, is exactly what you are here to learn. Tomorrow you will discover part of the answer to your question," Godmother replied. "Hurry now, I think Pantry Door has something wonderful for us to eat when we are finished here."

The rest of the afternoon, Godmother and Belinda talked about Cinderella's childhood and finished all the rest of the daily chores and enjoyed a wonderful supper.

The next day, after cleaning and dusting, Godmother took out a bucket, cinder shovel, and small broom and led Belinda to the fireplace.

"Well, time to learn more about your mother and how she became a real princess," Godmother began. "Your mother was a true princess even though she did not have servants and a palace."

She scooped some ashes up in the shovel and dumped them into the bucket. "Here, you try. Mind you—do not let the ashes scatter.

The *slightest* movement of air will send ashes all over the room." Belinda took the shovel and swept ashes into it with the small broom. "How can that be, Fairy Godmother? How can anyone be a real Princess and not have a palace and servants?" Belinda asked.

"My dear child, your mother endured many hardships all the while remaining a sweet, loving child. In her heart, she knew she must continue learning and growing stronger with each lesson the days presented to her. She worked hard and never complained; she was always thoughtful of others, even to her stepsisters who were very mean to her." "What is a sweet and loving child like?" asked Belinda. "How long do I have to have daily lessons? Why can't I learn them at home?"

"All good questions, Belinda," Godmother replied. "You need to experience and observe what a sweet, loving person is like. Daily lessons will continue just as long as it takes. Everyone learns at a different pace. Your life in the palace was *not* offering you many opportunities to learn about real, everyday life. Every good leader must understand what the daily lives of his or her subjects are like. What do you think you should do to learn about your people and their lives?"

"Oh, I get it! I am here to learn about things I could not experience without servants always doing *everything* for me. I guess I have to try living like most other children live. Right, Godmother?"

"Right you are, dear child. And it takes experiencing many, many daily life events. You also were not very appreciative of your easy life and your wonderful family." Godmother paused and smiled at her. "There is so much more to come," she continued, "you have made a little progress, Belinda. Be patient, I promise your life here will be interesting and at times very exciting. Let's finish up here, have a bath and take our supper in front of a cozy fire in our freshly cleaned fireplace."

Each of the next few days was nearly the same routine. Godmother would leave for short periods of time. When she returned, she could see how Belinda was doing and what she had learned about being on her own and how to work. Belinda always found a little note to teach her any new task. And now that Belinda had mastered the daily chores, Godmother decided it was time to give the *would-be princess* a few new experiences.

The Kitten

The next morning, as the bright, sunny day dawned, Belinda's fairy godmother awakened her with breakfast in bed.

"Wake up, my little dear," Fairy Godmother sang out. "See what I have for you."

Belinda rolled over, sat up, and rubbed her eyes, "What is it?" She fluffed up her two pillows and leaned back on them, a smile brightening her face.

"Breakfast in bed. And it's your favorite!" Godmother sat the tray across Belinda's lap and tucked a napkin into the neck of her nightgown. "You have been so helpful around the house, I thought it was time for a small reward. Do you like it?"

Belinda's eyes grew wide and her mouth dropped open. "Wow! Godmother! It's my most favorite breakfast. Strawberries and cream with scones and tea." She began to eat, using her good table manners. At the second bite she stopped and grinned. "Thank you so very much, Godmother!"

"You are very welcome, Belinda. While you eat, I want to tell you something. I have been called away on important fairy godparent business. Several of us are needed to help a family in trouble." She watched Belinda's face to see if she was listening. Belinda nodded and continued eating.

"I must ask you to do the usual chores by yourself today. I hope you can do them all by suppertime. Can I count on you?" Godmother asked.

Belinda's face grew serious. She started to protest, then thought a moment. She crinkled her brow. *Maybe this is a princess lesson day*, she thought. "Well, I'm not sure I can do them all," she said. "Since I've been here I have worked hard. At least I'm too busy to be bored. But—"

Godmother's eyebrows twitched up a notch. "But what, Belinda?"

"But I do get sort of tired of being alone. I miss having more people around. Will you be gone the whole day?"

"Yes, but I'll be back for supper." Godmother's twinkling lights appeared and soon nearly covered all of her. "I must be off, dear. They are calling me. Perhaps I can do something about your loneliness. Too-ta-loo!" she sang out, then gave a little wave and was gone from view.

Belinda finished her breakfast in bed, being careful not to get any stains or spills on her nightdress and bedding. "I'll start with the kitchen and my breakfast dishes. Then I'll work on cleaning the floors. And then I will do the dusting and make my bed last." She hummed a little tune her mother had taught her and put on the clothes Godmother had given her for housework. She tied on her blue apron just like her godmother's, and headed for the kitchen with the breakfast tray.

By lunchtime, she was nearly finished sweeping the floors with her little broom. She knocked on Pantry Door and asked, "What do you have for me today, Pantry Door?" "Today," Pantry Door said, "you are working very hard. How would you like to have meatloaf, macaroni and cheese, salad, and milk? I might even have a little ice cream for you. What kind is your favorite?"

"I could eat all that and a big dish of chocolate ice-cream, if you please, Mr. Door!" Belinda called over her shoulder as she washed her hands, preparing for lunch.

"It pleases me very much to give you lunch," Pantry Door said. "It is ready when you are." With that, the door opened. On the lowest shelf of the pantry was the hot lunch just as the door had promised.

Belinda took her lunch to the kitchen table and sat down to eat and chat with the door, as was now her habit. When she finished she said, "Thank you" to the door, washed and dried the dishes, and replaced them in the cupboard.

"Now, to finish the floors, and dust. That will leave just enough time to sweep my room, make my bed, and rest before Godmother returns."

Belinda was a little slow finishing the floor and even slower dusting. She enjoyed playing with the pretty glass figurines on the living room table and turning the lamps on and off as she dusted the shades. Polishing the tables was her favorite chore since it gave her a reason to look at herself in the shiny surfaces. "Now, for my bed. I'll really surprise Godmother and do it perfectly this time," Belinda said aloud. She puffed the soft pillows. She tucked in the edges of the sheet. Then she lifted up the white coverlet by the end and gave it a flip, the way she had seen Fairy Godmother do it. The quilt settled lightly upon the bed, but it wasn't smooth. Belinda spied a big lump right in the middle of her bed. She lifted the quilt and flipped it again. It settled, but the lump was still there.

What is that? she wondered. *Did I leave my nightdress under the sheet?* She crawled across the bed and began to pat the lump. The lump moved! She patted again. This time the lump grew four other little peaks. She patted it again, a bit harder. Now the lump moved and growled. Belinda jumped back and screamed, "Help! There's something in my bed!"

The lump moved toward a pillow, and disappeared under it. Belinda circled the bed, her hands safely behind her back. "Who are you? You'd better answer me, I'm a princess, you know." There was no sound from the pillow. She circled the bed again. "You better come out or I'll take my broom and pound you out. I know you are hiding under my pillows. Come out!" she demanded.

All at once a dark thing darted out from under the pillow, jumped off the bed, and ran under it. Belinda got down on her hands and knees and peeked under the dust ruffle. Two bright yellow eyes looked back at her. Belinda trembled. She tried to be brave, but she was pretty frightened. In her loudest voice she shouted, "Come out at once! I'll really use the broom and sweep you out! Are you a mouse? A bunny?"

Gathering her courage, Belinda reached her broom toward the yellow eyes and wiggled it slightly. Suddenly a small animal pounced on the broom straws.

"Oh," she said as she pulled the broom from under the bed. "It's a kitten! You're a baby kitten. Here kitty, kitty," she called in a high, sweet voice.

The kitten scampered out from under the bed and up under the covers again. Belinda could see the lump moving all around on the bed. Then it stopped and remained very still. "I know, you want to play," Belinda cried. "Oh good, let's play.

She lightly scratched the covers and the kitten pounced right where her fingers had been. "You silly kitten! You can't catch me!" Belinda quickly threw off the covers and sheets.

The kitten was so surprised it arched its back and hissed at her. "You are not very scary but aren't you cute!" Belinda cooed.

The kitten's yellow eyes were framed by dark lines that pointed to the pinkest nose Belinda had ever seen. There were stripes of black and gray on the kitten's back and tail, and snowy white socks on its feet. It had a fuzzy white chest and white tips on its tail and ears.

The kitten calmly sat down—just as most cats do in the middle of play—and began to lick its paws, looking bored. Belinda sat down on the bed slowly and reached out carefully to touch the kitten's soft, furry head.

"My goodness, but you are a tiny thing. You're no longer than my hand. And listen to you. You can hum a little song. Well, you have a pink ribbon around your neck so, I think I'll call you Melody. Would you like some milk, Melody?" She reached for the kitten to carry it to the kitchen.

The kitten hissed, swatted her hand, and ran under the pillow to hide.

"Ouch! You little brat! That hurt! You have little daggers in those tiny paws. Look, I have a scratch and it hurts." Belinda dabbed at the scratch with the corner of her apron. "You are not a very nice kitten," she whimpered.

Pantry Door called out, "Come see what I have. I have something for your new friend, Belinda. I have ointment and a small bandage for your scratch too."

Belinda went to the door as it opened. "What do you have?" she asked. "Why should we give that naughty kitten anything? See this scratch?"

"Put the salve and bandage on your scratch," Pantry Door said. "Remember, the kitten is just a frightened baby. Take this little bowl of warm milk. Set it by the bed and see if the kitten comes out to drink it."

"Still, I don't know if I want to give that bad kitty anything. It should not have hurt me. I was only trying to play with it," Belinda whined.

"The kitten does not know you. It is only protecting itself," Pantry Door explained. "You will have to win its trust and love."

"Oh, all right. I'll try. But it had better not scratch me again."

Belinda carried the bowl of warm milk to the edge of her bed. The kitten scampered from under the pillow and dived under the bed. Belinda set the bowl on the floor and lay down beside it. Two yellow eyes stared at her. She stared back. Belinda stared, the kitten stared. Before she knew it, she dozed off waiting for the kitten to come out.

"Well, what do we have here?" Godmother's voice startled Belinda awake.

Belinda quickly sat up and cried, "The kitten. Where is it?"

"Settle down my dear. Why were you sleeping on the floor? What is this bowl doing here?" Godmother asked with a chuckle.

"The milk is gone!" Belinda wailed. "It was for the kitten. It scratched me and Pantry Door said it was afraid, so I was going to make it trust me by feeding it and—"

Godmother held up her hand. "Slowly, quietly. Tell me about the kitten. Where did you find it?" She sat on the floor beside Belinda and inspected her scratch.

"In my bed. It was hiding in my bed!" Belinda jumped up and began to pound the covers. "Come out, you silly kitten. Come out at once! I am the Princess and must be obeyed."

"Dear, dear, that will never do." Godmother shook her head. "The kitten will only become more frightened if you pound on the bed. It's never heard of a princess and has no use for one. We had better try something else."

Belinda folded her arms across her chest. "What do you know about kittens? It's a mean little beast. I hate it!" She shouted.

"Belinda, have you ever had a pet before?" Godmother asked.

"What's a pet?" Belinda snarled.

"Well, a pet is something you enjoy petting or stroking. Usually it's an animal to play with or keep around for company. But animals have rules of their own and we humans have to learn them. If we treat animals kindly and respect their rules, some of them become our friends and playmates," Godmother explained.

"I make the rules," Belinda cried. "That's what a real ruler does."

Godmother laughed. "Not yet, my dear. You have a great deal to learn about the world before you can make rules. Here's a little book that will tell you all about the rules of cats and kittens." Godmother took a small book out of her dress pocket.

Belinda grabbed the book and threw it across the room. "You know I can't read. I'm a Princess. People read to me."

"Can't read? That will never do. You must begin your school lessons very soon then. But for the time being, I've given this book a voice." She magically transported the book back from the corner where it had landed. "You sit here for a while and listen to the book. I'll get us some supper from Pantry Door. I'm hungry."

When Godmother came back to get Belinda for supper, she found her sitting in the middle of the bed. The kitten was on her lap, purring. "Oh, look, Godmother, the kitten likes to have me pet it."

"My, my! How did you manage that?" Godmother sat gently on the foot of the bed so she did not scare the kitten.

"Easy! I just followed kitten rules. The book told me what to do." Belinda giggled loudly. The kitten jumped and scurried under the pillow. "Oh, I forgot. When a kitten is in a strange place, it does not like loud noises or fast moves." She sat very still and waited. The kitten poked its head out from behind the pillow. Its eyes were very big and its hair stood on end. Belinda moved her hand ever so slowly and wiggled a finger at the kitten. It jumped at her finger, but this time the kitten did not scratch her. She began to stroke its fur and the kitten sat on her lap.

"That's amazing, Belinda. Why did the kitten do that?" Godmother asked.

"Kittens are more curious than frightened—most of the time. And the book said this kitten is about ten weeks old. It's just a baby. If I do the right things for it, it will think I am its mother and trust me. Isn't that funny?"

Godmother reached out and stroked the kitten. "Do you want to be the kitten's mother? You would have to be *completely* responsible for it. I do not have time to care for a kitten."

Belinda looked up from the kitten. "What does *be responsible for a kitten* mean, Godmother?"

"Well," Godmother counted on her fingers. "You will give the kitten its food. You will brush its hair to keep it clean and healthy. You will clean up any messes it makes. If it is sick, you will nurse it back to health."

Belinda clapped her hands. The kitten ran under the pillow. "I can do all of that. I *am* the kitten's mother. I have named her Melody because she hums little songs when she is happy. The kitten ran out from under the pillow and squatted for a moment on the white coverlet.

"Well, little mother," Godmother laughed. "Here is your first mess to clean up. The kitten just wet on your bed."

Belinda made a face and said, "Bad, bad, Melody! Shame on you!" The kitten ran under the bed. "Why did the kitten do that?" Belinda moaned.

"Because it's a baby and doesn't know any better. Also, it will need a proper place to go when it needs to. Quickly, get a towel and some water. You'll have to sponge the wet spot before it leaves a stain."

"Oh, no. I don't do that sort of cleaning. Godmother, why don't you just magic it away?" Belinda begged.

"Magic can be used for many things. When I was given my magical powers I learned the rules that come with the power. First, I try not to use my magic when someone is learning. I must never use it to interfere with someone's life lessons. Second, you are the kitten's new mother, so the responsibility for the kitten yours. That is one of your life lessons, to become responsible. Better bring the towels quickly. The longer you take, the harder it will be to clean."

Belinda fetched towels and water and cleaned the wet spot made by Melody. Then Godmother had her put a little white vinegar on the spot so it would not stain and make the scent go away.

"Do you know why we must get rid of the scent of the kitten's wet spot?" Godmother asked.

"The book said that a cat or kitten would always return to its own scent. And it will repeat the act that caused the scent. My goodness, I hope we got it all out. I really do not want Melody wetting on my bed again."

"Well, let's see what the book says to give the kitten for its toilet. Godmother thumbed through the book. "Here it is. It says the kitten will always go to a clean, dry box of sand or dirt for a toilet. While your baby takes a nap, let's get the box ready."

Belinda skipped along behind her Fairy Godmother. "What else does Melody need, Godmother? We might as well do it all at once. Does my baby kitten need clothes or shoes?"

Godmother's laughter sounded like the tinkle of wind chimes. "Goodness, no! It was born with a wonderful furry coat that keeps it both warm and cool depending upon the temperature. And its little feet are well padded for walking on almost anything. But what a thoughtful little mother you are to ask." They found a suitable litter box, filled it with sand and put it in a corner of the bathroom. Then Belinda and Godmother sat down to supper and asked the cat book to read aloud to them as they ate.

Just as they were finishing their meal, the kitten suddenly jumped up on the table and began to drink milk out of Belinda's glass. Belinda squealed with delight. The squeal frightened kitten and it jumped again, knocking over the glass of milk. Then it ran through the dish of gravy leaving tiny paw prints all over the clean, white tablecloth.

Before Belinda could catch her kitten, it turned over a vase of flowers, which broke several dishes as it fell. Belinda made a grab for the kitten and it jumped to the edge of the tablecloth. As it hung there hissing, the tablecloth slowly slid off the table, and all of the food dishes went crashing to the floor.

Godmother and Belinda sat dazed for a moment. In an instant the kitten had turned their supper table into a disaster, and now Belinda's baby was nowhere to be seen. Godmother started to laugh and Belinda joined in. They laughed until tears filled their eyes.

Then Belinda began to moan, "Oh, no! Oh, no, no, no!"

"My, my! Whatever is the matter, Belinda?" Fairy Godmother asked.

"The mess. Just look at this terrible mess and it's all mine to clean up!" Belinda covered her face with both hands and continued moaning.

Without a word, Godmother began to clear the broken glass. Belinda reluctantly joined her.

"Work is always easier if we sing, Godmother offered. "Here's a little tune that helps me when I'm tired. *"One, two, three, just look at me. Dancing and prancing along. Four, five, six, this is easy to fix. Let's sing our working song."*

In a remarkably short time, all the broken dishes were in the trash and the kitchen was clean and spotless again.

Belinda and Godmother sat down at the table to drink the iced punch Pantry Door had waiting for them when they had finished their work.

After several big gulps of punch, Belinda asked, "Godmother, why did you help me clean up after my kitten? You didn't have to. It was my responsibility."

Godmother's face grew serious. "What an excellent question, my dear. Why do you think I helped?"

"I think because you wanted to help me and you knew it was a very big mess. Too big for me to do alone. But why didn't you magic it done?" Belinda asked.

"It would have been easier to use magic, which is true. But sometimes easier is not best. I told you I only use my magic when I believe it is allowed. You are *learning* how to work, and how to be responsible for your adopted baby kitten. You are also learning to be joyful, even when the job is hard, just as your mother did. Sharing burdens with those you love is part of life. These life lessons are much too important to be magically done away with. You learn best by doing."

Belinda cocked her head to the side and asked, "what does adopted mean, Godmother?"

"It means," Fairy Godmother said, "that you have *agreed* to act as if the kitten were your own child. You promise to care for the kitten's well-being, to be responsible for it."

"Well-being? What's that supposed to mean?"

Godmother sighed and sat down. "Well-being means about what the words say, *being well*, safe, and comfortable. It means you look after your kitten's needs just as if you were her real mother. You see that she has food and water. You keep her warm when it's cold. You teach her what's right and what's wrong. And if she gets sick—you give her treatment and comfort her until she gets well. Beyond that you love her very, very, much."

"Godmother," Belinda asked with a puzzled look on her face, "was I adopted?"

Fairy godmother chuckled and said, "Whatever gave you that idea?"

"Well, my mother and father try to provide all those things for me. They even have my special royal duties tutors for me."

"That is true," Godmother answered. "But you were *born* at the palace *to* your parents."

"Does that make me special?"

"You are indeed special. Adopted children are special too. They are chosen to be loved and cared for, just as you chose to love and care for your kitten. 'Adopt' means to take on the care or support of someone."

Belinda sat quietly for several minutes. "I certainly have learned a lot today."

"Tell me what you have learned," Godmother encouraged.

"Well, having a baby to take care of is not easy and not *all* fun. I learned that work could be fun, especially when it is shared. And singing helped too."

Godmother nodded.

Belinda continued, "Oh, yes, and I learned that kittens have rules of their own."

"Very good, Belinda. Shall we go see what your baby is up to now?"

"Melody? Where are you? Here kitty, kitty!" Belinda's voice sang out. "Are you hiding? Oh, Godmother come look! Melody is fast asleep in my bed."

Indeed, there was Melody, curled up right in the middle of the bed. Belinda lay down next to the kitten and stroked its fur ever so gently. In a blink of an eye, a tired Belinda was also asleep. Letting the two rest peacefully, Godmother fluttered her magic wand and Belinda was in her nightgown under the covers, with Melody on the pillow next to her head.

Fairy Godmother tucked the covers under Belinda's chin. "Sleep well, my little beauties. Today's lessons *were* a bit tiring." Godmother kissed the top of Belinda's head. "You'll need all of your strength for tomorrow's great adventure," she whispered and tiptoed out of the room.

The Stranger

The next morning after breakfast, Belinda and her kitten, Melody, went outside to play in a field in front of Godmother's cottage. Godmother said they could play outside in the fresh air, but when they saw a blue bird land on the fence it was time to come back inside. Belinda saw a big blue bird land on the fence.

"Come here, Melody. It's time for us to go in. That's enough hide-and-seek for today," Belinda called.

The kitten came bouncing through the grass meowing loudly. It was nearing lunchtime and Belinda's baby was obviously hungry. "Looks like rain," Belinda said as her eyes searched the darkening sky. "We had better hurry." She scooped up the kitten and started running toward the cottage. Just as she reached out to open the garden gate, a scruffy-looking man dressed in odd clothing stepped in front of the gate. Belinda stopped.

The stranger smiled. "Well, isn't that a cute little kitten. Can I pet him?"

Belinda pulled the hissing kitten closer to her chest. "She doesn't like anyone but me. Who are you? Where did you come from?" A sense of fear caused a tightness in Belinda's tummy, and her heart began to race."

The man leaned on the gate, blocking Belinda from going to the house. "Oh, I live here in these woods. Name's Seth. You're a mighty pretty little girl. What's your name?"

"I'm the Princess, just visiting my fairy godmother. Do you know her?" "Sure, sure. I know everybody in these parts. You're a princess, you say?" He moved closer to Belinda. "Your mommy and daddy must be pretty rich."

"Very rich," Belinda replied. "We are royalty. Please, move away from the gate. It might rain and I don't want my kitten to get wet."

"You're to come with me." The man held out a slip of paper. "See, I got a note from your godmother. Here read it!" He forced the note into Belinda's hand, and before she realized what was happening he grabbed Melody by the back of the neck and held her up above Belinda's reach. "If you want your kitten, you come follow me." He walked a few steps away from the gate. "Come on, Miss Princess. You follow me."

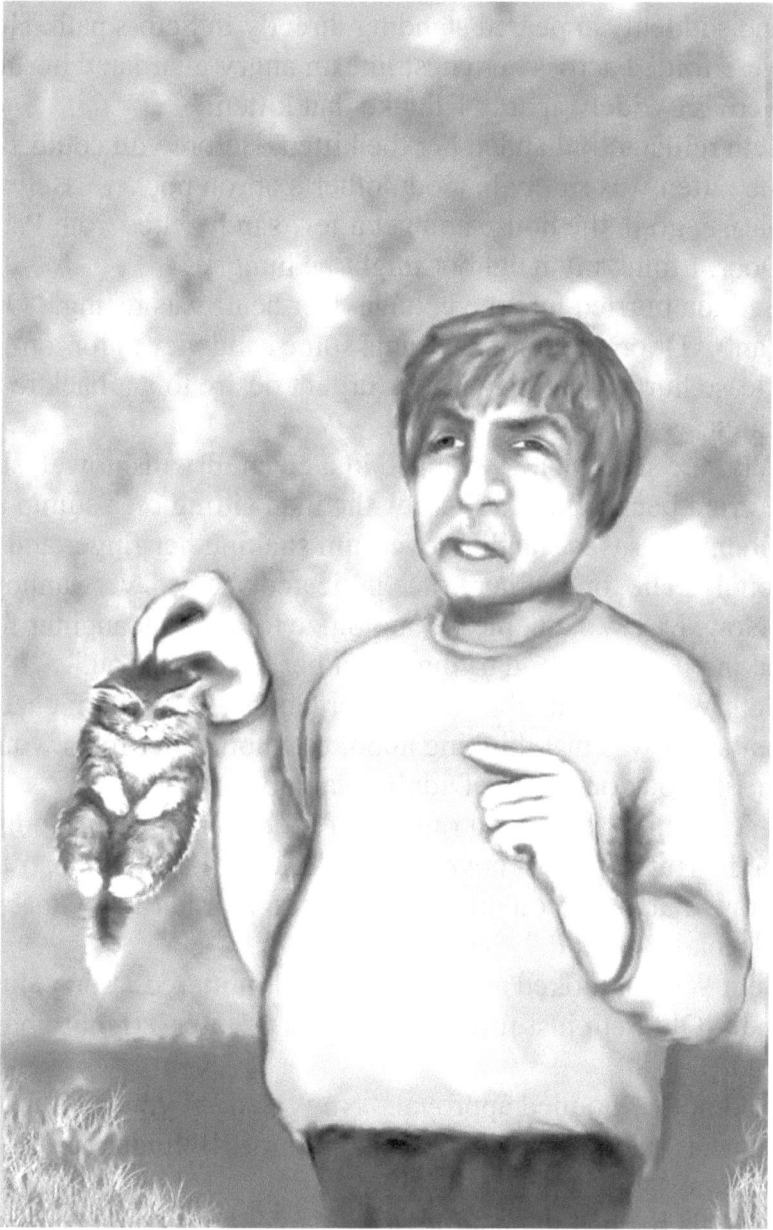

"Follow you where, Seth Wilson?" Fairy Godmother asked. She had suddenly appeared standing directly in Seth's path. Her arms were folded across her chest like an angry guard and her feet were set widely apart. "I'll take that kitten."

Seth reluctantly handed her the kitten. Before you could say "it" the kitten was safely in Godmother's apron pocket. "Belinda, please, go in the house and get a few sandwiches from Pantry Door. I think my neighbor might be hungry."

Belinda hurried into the cottage. Her heart was racing. "Quick, Pantry Door. Godmother wants some sandwiches for a neighbor. Please hurry!" Belinda felt an urgent desire to get back to her kitten.

With the sandwiches wrapped in a clean, dry dishtowel, she hurried back outside. She saw the man sitting on a stump and Godmother was standing over him shaking her finger and talking loudly. The tone of her voice indicated she was very annoyed.

"Now, Mr. Wilson, please apologize to my goddaughter for taking her kitten and trying to get her to follow you."

Seth Wilson seemed to wilt under Godmother's stern gaze. "Yes, ma'am. I was just thinking about the money her folks would give me if I took her home. Didn't mean no harm."

"Yes, Seth. I know you run out of food sometimes," Godmother said. "But you must never, ever take what is not yours. You know that! And you must never frighten or harm anyone, especially a child."

Seth Wilson looked at the ground and muttered, "sorry, little miss. Old Seth just forgot his manners. Had no right to bother you."

Godmother nodded approval. "Now, Seth, if you need food and can't get work, you come talk to me. Belinda, please give him the sandwiches."

Belinda handed the bundle of food over the gate, keeping the gate between her and the frightening man.

"Thank you kindly." Mr. Wilson took the food and walked away down the path toward the woods.

Godmother opened the gate and handed the trembling kitten to Belinda. "My dear, we must have a little talk. Let's go inside. It's starting to rain."

They went inside and sat on cushions in front of the fire. The kitten drank some broth and was soon asleep on Belinda's lap. Godmother spoke softly, "Belinda, didn't your mother and father tell you *not* to talk to strangers?"

Belinda shook her head. "Well, no, Godmother, there are no strangers at the castle. Everyone knows me and I know them. Why was Mr. Wilson so mean to me and Melody?"

Godmother was quiet for a long time. " People have different habits, they do not behave the way most of us do. Some people do not respect others, and sometimes do them harm. It is important that you understand that you cannot trust others until they *earn* the trust. Just like the kitten did not trust you right away. I think we should make a rule."

"A rule?" Belinda asked. "Like kitten rules and the laws in my village, in Grandfather's kingdom?"

"Something like that. Because you are a young child and do not yet know the ways of *all* people, we will make a rule that you are *not* to talk to any strangers. A stranger is someone you don't know. They have not earned your parent's trust or yours. And you must never go with somebody you do not know and trust. Do you understand?"

Belinda said, "I think so, Godmother. That *awful*-looking man really scared me and my kitten. I won't go with scary-looking people for sure. What should I have done?"

"Not every *mean* stranger will *look* awful. Not every awful looking person is mean. One thing you could have done was trust your feelings. The moment you felt even a tad bit of fear, you should have run to get me, or run for safety. Be alert while you are playing; notice if someone comes by. Move to a safe place, like the yard or the house, or call me. It's a good idea, while you are here, not to go so far into the meadow to play."

Belinda said, "Oh, I remember. Mother told me never to leave the palace grounds without a grown-up. She thought I might get lost. And I remember hearing once about a little boy who got lost in the mountains."

"A lost or injured child is a parent's greatest worry. So our rules are … ?" Godmother quizzed.

Belinda answered, "Be alert. Keep a watch out for any kind of stranger. If I feel fearful—run to safety. Don't go far from home or the sight of a *trusted* grown-up. Don't go with anyone I don't know."

Godmother chuckled. "Very good! People who *really* love you will *not* harm you. But we don't know *anything* about strangers."

"But Mr. Wilson had my baby and I'm supposed to keep Melody safe and he said he knew you, Godmother." Belinda's words tumbled out in a rush. "I thought he was a friend of yours. How was I to know he might hurt me?"

"Seth Wilson is not a friend, but I do know him. The best way to help Melody was to run to get me. You didn't know he could not be trusted, but your *fear* was trying to tell you he might hurt you. Here's what we'll do: we'll pick a magic word. Only those people whom we know we *can trust* will know the secret word." Godmother smiled. "You choose our secret magic word."

Belinda thought and thought. Finally she said, "I love the sound of melon. It feels funny in my mouth when I say it. Melon, melon, melon. It even sounds like Melody. That's it, 'melon' is my secret magic word!"

Godmother frowned. "How do you spell melon?"

"How should I know?" Belinda shrugged. "Why does it matter how melon is spelled?"

"Well, what if I must send a note to you with our secret word. You will need to read it. Melon is spelled like it sounds in your mouth. Godmother pronounced the word slowly, "*m e l o n.*"

Belinda understood now. "Oh! If I can't read our secret word, and if just anyone reads the note *to* me, they might say our secret word and use it and maybe tell me to come with them."

"Right you are, my dear. And someone *like* Mr. Wilson might read my note for you." Godmother shook her head from side to side. "We don't want that."

Belinda swallowed hard. "Godmother, I think I had better start my reading lessons right away."

"Good!" Godmother danced delightedly. "I just happen to have a surprise for you. Put the kitten on the pillow and follow me."

They left the warming fire and walked to the front of the house. Belinda noticed for the first time a door to the left of the front door. There were letters on it. "What do the letters say?" Belinda asked.

Godmother pointed to each letter. She pronounced each letter carefully, "*s-c-h-o-o-l-*, spells school. I've created a lovely school for you and some new friends."

Belinda opened the door and peeked inside. The room was filled with bright colors. The walls were a happy peach. The lights hanging from the ceiling were all shaped like stars. The three table desks were painted bright red, and there were three unusual desk chairs. Each chair was a different bright color. The floor was a cool, forest green. At the front of the room was a green chalkboard; a piece of chalk was moving itself across the board writing the alphabet in big pink letters.

"What do you think?" Godmother asked. "Do you like this classroom?"

"It is very pretty, Godmother. But there is no teacher and I see three desks. I had a royal tutor at the palace. This isn't a real schoolroom, is it? My study room was full of books and it was dull, not bright like this one."

Godmother danced a little jig and twirled her wand. "It is a magic schoolroom. Everything in the room can move and talk. There will be two other students. I will provide you the best teacher for a student princess. Would you like to start school tomorrow? You can meet your new classmates then."

"This *might* be fun. How many other students?" asked Belinda as she touched one of the desks. "Do I know them?" She thought of her only young friends, children of palace servants, and how she missed their exciting play.

"No, you do not know them. You can meet them tomorrow morning. School can be great fun, Belinda. The other two children also have not yet learned to read and write, so I invited them to come to this school. Well then, let's get working, you will need extra time to prepare for tomorrow and a little extra sleep tonight. There is also some hard work in school."

"What kind of hard work, Godmother?" Belinda asked.

"*Noodle* hard work." Godmother tapped the side of her head. "You will have to use that wonderful brain of yours. Don't worry, you have all it takes to do the *noodle* work."

The Classroom

Bright and early the next morning, Belinda bounded out of bed and ran to the kitchen to have her breakfast. She was very excited about meeting the other children and starting school.

Godmother was sitting at the table reading and drinking hot peach tea. "Godmother, I'm in a hurry to go to school," Belinda said.

She began to eat the breakfast, which was already waiting for her. "Will I need books or pencils?"

"No, my dear. But you need to tidy your dishes and tend to your kitten before school." Godmother peeked over the book she held. "School begins at eight-thirty sharp. Better hurry."

Belinda protested, "I'm sure I will not have time to do my dishes and feed the kitten. What time is it?"

"It's already eight o'clock," Godmother said, continuing to sip her tea and read. She looked at Belinda when she had finished eating. "Better hurry, the first student is already in the schoolroom."

"But I don't want to do chores. I want to go play with the other children. I want to learn to read." Belinda's lower lip came out into her angry, spoiled, princess pout.

Godmother said not a word. From time to time she would glance at the clock and tap her finger in time with the loud tick-tock sound it made.

"Oh, all right," Belinda gave in. Quick as a bunny, Belinda washed her dishes, made her bed, fed her kitten, and washed her hands and face before rushing to the schoolroom. To her surprise, she had finished her work so quickly, she was actually a bit early. The large, brass bell with a black handle was ringing itself. The clock in the classroom called out, "eight-twenty-five in the morning. Five minutes until class begins."

A dark-haired boy sat at one of the desks. He was dressed in short, white pants, leather sandals, and a green shirt with white stripes at the edge of the collar, neck, and sleeves. His shining skin was the color of polished pecan shells.

Belinda called to her godmother. "Godmother, come here quickly. There is a *peculiar* person in my schoolroom. He looks terribly different."

Godmother appeared beside Belinda. She beamed at the boy who now stood and looked at them. "This is Juan Garcia. He has traveled a very long distance to study here. Juan, this is my Goddaughter, Belinda."

Juan smiled and said, "I am most pleased to meet you, Belinda. My full name is Juan Eduardo Garcia."

Belinda tilted her head to one side. "What did he say? It sounded funny." Then looking at Juan she said, "You may call me Your Highness. I'm the Princess. Everybody knows that."

Belinda's fairy godmother began to shake from head to toe causing little sparks to fly in all directions. "Belinda, there will be none of that 'Princess' business here. Juan is our guest. You will use your best manners with him and the other student. Do you understand me?"

"But he's dressed so funny and he sounds odd. Besides, who asked him to be in my school room anyway?" Belinda stomped out of the room and ran headlong into another child. "And who are you?" She demanded.

The short girl dressed in blue bibs caught her balance. "Boy! You nearly knocked me over. You're a beauty. I'll bet you can't milk a cow or ride a horse though. I live on a farm about two miles down the path. My father decided it was time for me to get my schooling. Fairy Godmother invited me to come for lessons with you."

"Well, you certainly are *not* the least bit pretty." Belinda had never seen anyone with such red hair and with red spots all over their face. "Who are you? What's that all over your face?" Belinda blurted out.

"Freckles. Where the sun kissed me, my mother says," the young girl laughed at Belinda's rude question.

"Belinda, this is Patsy Brown," Godmother said. "She is nearly twelve. Helping out on her family's farm has kept her from attending school. Both of you go into the classroom now and take your seats. Just for this morning, you may play games so that you three can get better acquainted. The games are in boxes and are waiting to instruct you about the game rules. Belinda, be on your best behavior."

Belinda opened her mouth to protest but decided to allow Godmother to leave before she let the other two children know just who was going to be the boss here. The classroom was for her, made by *her* fairy godmother. If Juan and Patsy were going to be allowed to share the special room, they had better be ready to obey her every wish and command. Sharing was not something Belinda's had yet learned to do.

Each child's desk had his or her picture and name on it so each knew where to sit.

Before Belinda could take over the class and give her first order, however, a game box flew to the center of the room. The three children were happily surprised by the animated game.

Belinda forgot all about taking over the classroom as the game instructed them on the rules. The first game was a funny word game. The person who drew the star token out of a box was told to say a funny word and then point to another person who must quickly say a word that rhymed with that word.

Game after game introduced itself. Belinda actually enjoyed playing with her new classmates. The entertainment was so much fun and changed so quickly, she forgot all about being the royal, bossy princess. Before they knew it, Godmother came into the room and announced it was time for the class to end.

"All right, children, I can see you have enjoyed your play day in the classroom. That's all for today. Please come back in the morning to begin your lessons and meet your teacher."

Juan and Patsy reluctantly went to meet their families waiting outside to take them home for the night. Belinda and Godmother finished the day with a few chores, discussed tomorrow's plans at supper, and then prepared for bed.

"Off to bed, Belinda. As I told you at supper, you will not have any chores other than your bed, dishes, and kitten while you are attending school."

"Goodnight, Godmother. I truly enjoyed playing the games with Patsy and Juan. I'll see you at breakfast."

Godmother sat alone in the kitchen for a few minutes. She had just summoned the best teacher in the world and could now rest assured that Belinda's life lessons would be exactly what she needed to become the royal Princess her family needed her to be."Tomorrow will be busy for all of us," she said. "Thank you my magical, little friends for all of your fine efforts with Belinda. Thanks to you, these children have a good start. Goodnight."

"Goodnight," echoed the pantry door, the talking clock, the notes, book, games, and all of Godmother's other magical helpers.

Belinda's New School

Godmother was sipping her usual morning tea when Belinda came running into the kitchen. "Where's my breakfast?" Belinda shouted. "I don't want to be late for the real first day of school. I made my bed perfectly. As soon as I have breakfast, I'll wash my dishes and put them away." Belinda stopped her jumping up and down long enough to notice that her place at the table was all set out with a fine breakfast.

"I am happy to see you are so eager for your first day in class. Your two new friends will be here shortly. Please, sit down and chew your food, Belinda. The class will begin at eight-thirty and only when all three of you are present." Godmother's scolding frown turned to a happy smile. "Now relax. You have more than half an hour before the class begins."

Belinda tried to eat more slowly and sit still but she had a secret plan and was eager to try it out. "I don't want to keep Patsy and Juan waiting. Where will you be, Godmother? Do you have another meeting or someone to help?" she asked very sweetly.

"I will finish my chores and be on my way to visit with your mother and father. They want a full report on your progress," Godmother said. "Is there a message you would like me to give them?"

"Just tell them I am doing fine. Can I talk to them in the mirror?" Belinda asked as she finished her breakfast and began washing the dishes.

"Well yes, anytime, but I have arranged for your class to visit your parents—today. They want to talk to you."

Belinda was not paying attention to Godmother's words; she was noisily putting away her breakfast dishes.

As Belinda was leaving the kitchen, Godmother called after her, "That's a fine job with your dishes, Belinda. Is that the school bell? I'll see you 'round about noon."

Belinda did not hear Godmother's last few words. She ran to the classroom shouting, "Juan, Patsy, where are you?" Now she would show them that she was a *real* princess. Finally, she would once again have others to give orders to and boss around. The classroom was as she remembered it.

Patsy and Juan were standing beside their chairs. "Look at this," Patsy called out. "Our desk chairs now have seat belts."

"Never mind that. You two just listen to me," Belinda spoke with the stern voice she had heard her grandfather, the King, use many times. "I am the boss of this class. I am a real-life princess so you two will have to obey me. Is that clear? What I say goes!" She stood with feet apart and hands on her hips. "Well, what's wrong with you? Why are you staring at me like that?"

"We aren't looking at you, Belinda." Juan pointed. "We are looking at the flashing sign on the chalkboard behind you. What does it say?"

"Silly, we can't read. I'll just ask it." She turned to the sign and asked, "What is your message, sign?" Before the words were out of her mouth, the flashing sign said, "Please sit in your chairs and buckle up. You will be taking a very fast ride. Buckle up."

The three children obediently strapped themselves into the chairs and sat with their hands folded in their laps. "What now?" Belinda shouted. "Why must we be strapped in?" Her chair began to move, as did the other chairs.

"That's why!" Patsy shouted. "These chairs are magic chairs! Woweeeee! We're goin' for a ride!"

Round and round, as if they were on a merry-go-round, the children rode in their chairs. Their whoops of glee bounced off the walls of the classroom.

"This is great fun!" Juan shouted. He folding his hands inside his chair and grinned ear-to-ear.

As suddenly as the ride began, it stopped and the children's chairs moved to form a semi circle around the center of the classroom. The floor in the middle of the circle began to smoke and glow. The children looked at each other with wide eyes, their mouths agape in wonder. Out of the smoke beamed a powerful blue light and from within that light appeared a shimmering figure that seemed to dance inside of the light.

Surely it couldn't be a real person, thought the children, because they could see right through the figure.

"I am the *teacher of all teachers*, Master Zhao, pronounced ZZZZ-OW," the figure said in a voice that sounded like low tones of music played on a giant pipe organ. "One who teaches must possess vast knowledge and wisdom. And you," he added, "my little Princess-to-be, you have but a smidgen of knowledge." Belinda was too awe-struck to reply. Her eyes got even bigger and her mouth clamped tightly shut. No one could take their eyes off the dazzling image.

"One who teaches must have more than knowledge and wisdom. A teacher must live the truths they teach." The blue beam of light faded into the floor and the three children could now see what proved to be a solid person, a man. He seemed old but youthful. His white hair looked like it was flying upward, pushed by an unseen force like static electricity made by rubbing a balloon on hair. The teacher, dressed in a flowing, black robe trimmed in scarlet, walked around the circle looking into each child's face as he spoke.

The Teacher of All Teachers

"Please, tell me your name and what each of you has come here to learn. Be brief and speak from the heart," the Teacher of All Teachers stood before Patsy and pointed to her. Patsy was not a bit afraid. She answered in a clear voice,

" I am Patsy Brown. My family is a poor, farm family. I have not been able to attend school because I am needed to help with the work. I have been wishing to learn about the world and the new things—inventions and technology—that will help my family to be happier and earn a better living. Godmother heard my wish and invited me to attend this special school."

The teacher nodded and moved to stand before Juan and pointed at him. "And you? Please, tell me why you are here." Juan was a little shy but answered in a soft voice, "My name is Juan Eduardo Garcia. I, too, was invited by Godmother. My village is in need of many things. A lack of   education has held everyone there in a most difficult life. My people have sent me to learn all that I can, and then I will return to teach everyone else. I hope to be a teacher for my village."

"Excellent," the teacher said, "and how about you?" He stood before Belinda and pointed his long finger at her. "Please, tell me your reason for coming to this special classroom."

Belinda had never seen anyone like the powerful teacher. She did not know whether to be afraid or angry. She decided to try out her angry voice. Sitting up very tall she replied,

"Well, sir, I am a princess, you know—Princess Belinda. And by the way, just so you know, I do *not* take orders. I am here to learn to read, Godmother says I should. And I want to learn quickly what is necessary to become the ruler of my people. I will rule an entire kingdom."

"Well," the teacher put his hands behind his back and paced back and forth in front of Belinda "you also have an important reason for being here. However, please think about this: no one in my class is considered more important or better than anyone else. Also, young lady, all of you students will use your best manners, best behavior, and most respectful attitude. And I, as your master teacher will do the same. If anyone here does not want to abide by these basic rules of the classroom, raise your hand now."
Juan and Pasty held their hands in their laps and did not make a move. Belinda wiggled and started to raise her hand. But an odd thing happened; she felt her heart beat very fast and a peculiar, happy feeling tingled through her whole body. She, too, folded her hands, showing she would accept the rules set forth by the teacher.
"Good! Now let me preview the way your lessons will be given. The teacher pulled a laser pointing stick out of his sleeve and drew a circle on the floor in front of the children. "This shall become our life teaching theater. We will be able to observe people and events in all parts of the world and we will be able to visit places by going *into* this magical theater. It is the most efficient and thorough way to absorb your lessons. What do you say, shall we test drive this wonderful device?"
"Oh, yes!" cried all three children at the same time.
"Please remember these things: you must stay in your chairs with the seatbelt fastened securely; you must only leave your chair when all movement has stopped. And when we are observing, we must be absolutely silent." The blue light beamed up through the floor again and the teacher stepped into the middle of it. "Clear?"
"Clear!" shouted Patsy, Juan and Belinda.
"Let's give it a test!" Patsy shouted.
While the children were experiencing their new traveling theater classroom, Godmother was visiting with Cinderella, the Prince, and King. The four of them had been watching through the magic mirror, as the children were introduced to their teacher and their classroom.

"Oh, Godmother, how I wish I would have had a school and teacher like that," said Cinderella. "Belinda is such a fortunate little girl."

The Prince and King agreed. "I have no doubt the lessons will *completely* prepare our little princess to become the kind and wise ruler my kingdom deserves. These are good people who live and work here," the King declared. "I am forever grateful to you, Godmother. But how long do you think Belinda will be staying with you?"

"Yes, please, Godmother, we want Belinda to come home. And she appears to have greatly changed. I believe she is a much improved person now," Cinderella said.

"I believe she really should come home to you *when* she has learned her lessons of the heart, and becomes a real princess. But if she *sincerely* desires to return home, she may do so. You are right, she is much easier to live with now," said Godmother with a sly smile. "However, if she returns home too soon, she will likely revert to the same old behavior.

"Well, we will discuss that later," said the Prince. "What's behind that smile, Godmother?"

"I have arranged with the other parents and the teacher for you to have a visit with the three children—right here. Are you ready to serve lunch to your guests? They should be whizzing in here in about an hour."

The surprised King quickly ordered a banquet to be prepared at once. Cinderella and the Prince put on their best clothes and stood with the King and Godmother in the great banquet hall excitedly awaiting their guests' arrival. Just then they heard the distant chatter and laughter of children. They looked in the direction of the voices above their heads. Chairs and children and a teacher were slowly descending to the banquet room floor.

"Please, do not leave your chairs until all motion has stopped," called out the teacher. "Take your time to catch your balance. It was a very fast trip."

Cinderella and the Prince ran to embrace their daughter. She was laughing and looked happier than they had ever seen her.

"Oh, Mother and Daddy, we could see you in our classroom's circle theater. And I knew we were coming to lunch with you before *you* knew," Belinda said excitedly. "Just wait till you hear about all the things we have seen and the places we have been today!"

"Belinda, this is a good time for you to practice your best manners," the teacher quietly coached her. "Please, introduce your guests to your family."

Belinda walked up to her teacher. "Mother, Father, Grandfather, this is our new teacher. He is The Teacher of All Teachers. We are to call him Master Zhao." She was surprised to see that her parents made a slight bow to the teacher, and the King nodded his head showing a rare sign of respect. She went on, "And these are my new friends and classmates, Patsy Brown and Juan Garcia. Master Zhao, Juan, Patsy, this is my family, the King—my Grandfather, the Crown Prince and Princess—my Father and Mother."

"Golly! You really are a Princess," Patsy blurted out, then clapped her hand over her mouth. "Ooops! Sorry."

Master Zhao cleared his throat and said, "a princess in training." Everyone laughed and began to talk all at once.

The old King shouted above the happy noise of the reunion, "Come, children, you must be very hungry! We can talk and enjoy food at the same time." He and the teacher walked behind the joyful group, herding them toward the table and the delicious food awaiting them. Patsy and Juan could hardly believe their eyes. They had never been in a castle nor had they seen a display of food quite so lavish. They followed Belinda and her parents to their appointed place at the table.

Once the servants began to put food on their plates, they watched the teacher to see how he was using the many silver forks, spoons, and knives. When gigantic dessert trays were brought to the table, everyone became admiringly quiet. Cakes, pies, puddings, cookies, ice cream, fruits, and cheeses tempted the guests.

"My tummy is so full, I wish I could start all over and have one of each kind of dessert," Juan declared.

"Me, too!" chimed in Patsy and Belinda. "Well, there is time to taste everything, just don't eat too much too fast," the Prince cautioned.

"We have serious planning to do," said Master Zhao. "Belinda, your parents have asked Fairy Godmother for a private talk with you. They have questions to ask you about staying with our class. I require parents' written permission for a student to be in my class. Juan and Patsy's parents have given their permission in writing. *If* you wish to stay in the class, your parents must give the same permission."

"If I wish to stay in the class with Patsy and Juan and you?" Belinda asked.

The Prince spoke up, "Your mother and I heard you one day while we viewed you in the magic mirror. You were asking to return to your home, leave Godmother's cottage."

"Yes, your father and mother miss you very much and want you to return home. They feel you have learned enough at Godmother's and should continue your lessons here with them," replied the teacher. "We will wait here for your family's final decision."

The Decision

Belinda, Cinderella, and the Prince left the merry group and went to Belinda's castle bedroom. As soon as she entered her elaborately furnished room, Belinda felt pangs of longing to return to her old life at the castle. Tears of wistfulness filled her eyes. "I really miss my home, Mother and Daddy. Maybe I *should* stay here," Belinda said.

"Well, Belinda, we have only a short time together right now to decide if you will rejoin your classmates on their learning adventures. We heard you say you wanted to come home one day. We see you *have* learned a great deal. Can you tell us what you would like to do now?" asked her father.

Before Belinda could reply, lights began to swirl like a tiny tornado in the corner of the room and Godmother's voice said, "Shouldn't I be in on this little discussion? It was my bargain with you and Belinda that started this—princess schooling." Godmother appeared, brushing sparkle dust off her shoulders and smiling.

"Godmother!" Cinderella cried. "you are just in time to help us with an important decision. We see that she has changed for the better. We wonder if it is time for Belinda to return home."

"It's true, what you have seen of your little princess and her changes in the magic mirror is a good *beginning*. You want her home. However, she has not learned *all* the lessons needed become an excellent leader and true princess. You see, she has quickly learned because of the *special* conditions at my cottage. Those conditions are not here," Godmother concluded.

"Godmother," Belinda ran to her and hugged her, "I don't know what to do. Yes, I did say I wanted to come back to the palace. And now I do feel like staying here. But the real fun at school is just beginning and I don't want to miss it. Please, please help me Godmother, what shall we do?"

"Yes, Godmother, what shall we do?" Asked Cinderella and

the Prince. "We want Belinda to finish her schooling right here—now that you have helped her understand the value of school and her life lessons."

Godmother quietly twirled her magic wand a moment or two and finally said, "I've got it! I know what we can do to make everyone happy."

"Tell us! What is your idea?" cried Belinda.

"Well, if your mother and father agree, we can arrange visits just like this through your teacher. He will bring you children here or bring your parents to your classroom. From time to time, your mother and father will also be able to observe you and your friends in your travel experiences. Observers must be silent, however. What do you think?" She studied Belinda's parents carefully. "How does that plan sound?"

Belinda's parents remained silent. Belinda clapped her hands, jumped up and down, and excitedly said, "I like it! Would that be okay with you?" She couldn't help dancing from one foot to the other anxious for their reply.

"What do you think, Cinderella?" the Prince asked. Shall we trust the wisdom of your Godmother? Will occasional visits and observations be enough to ease your motherly heart?"

"Maybe," Cinderella replied, "but tell me, Godmother, what will Belinda be doing and how will she learn the lessons of the heart?"

Godmother waved her wand and two of the children's magical chairs appeared. "Sit in these chairs and we'll give you a sample."

Cinderella and the prince sat down and looked expectantly at Godmother. "Fasten the seat belts. Away you go!" She smiled serenely at them.

Godmother and Belinda stood watching. The chairs whisked straight up and out of sight in an instant. "Don't worry, Belinda, they will be back quick as a wink with their answer. I am sure their decision will be what is truly best for you, aren't you?"

"Yes, Godmother. I believe so. They have certainly *tried* to do what is best for me. My goodness, here they are already." Cinderella and the Prince suddenly came into sight above their heads and slowly descended—coming to a standstill in front of Belinda and Godmother. They were laughing and talking excitedly.

"Mother, Daddy, what did you see? Wasn't it amazing?"

"Godmother, I don't know exactly how this works—we feel like we have been away for months yet the clock behind you says we were gone five minutes. Not only that, we saw events in *our* past, *our* future and we greeted people from many nations," the Prince exclaimed. "This is without a doubt the *best* teaching for our little princess."

"Yes, Belinda, now that I see how and what you have learned, you may go back to the schoolroom with your friends and Master Zhao," Cinderella said. "I know how you will learn. We observed you and Godmother as we were coming back, so I know how our observations will also work. Let us take a little more time to visit and tomorrow morning you may go and begin your true-life learning
adventures with your Teacher of all Teachers and your new friends. Let's join the others now."

"Oh, Mother, thank you!" Belinda hugged Cinderella with all her might. "I am so happy you have agreed. I know its right. Let's go tell Juan and Patsy I can go with them."

Once they were all gathered around the dining table, the others were told about the final decision to let Belinda go back to Godmother's house and the classroom. Patsy and Juan had already obtained their parents' agreement to spend the night at Belinda's palace. "Yes, children," Godmother said, "your *grandest* learning adventure will begin tomorrow. We leave here with the rising of the sun. Are you all ready?"

"Yes, yes, yes! Ready, set, go!" The three youngsters chanted.

"But Godmother, what about my baby kitten? What will I do about her tonight and when I am traveling in school?" Belinda asked. In all of the excitement, she had completely forgotten about Melody.

"You have a kitten, Belinda?" her father asked.

"Yes, and she takes very good care of it," Godmother replied. "Your kitten is fine for tonight. Master Zhao and I think you should take the kitten with you on your travels. I will prepare a little travel pack for Melody and fix it to the back of your chair. How does that sound? A classroom with a kitten?"

"Yes, yes! We want the kitten; we want the kitten," the children shouted.

"Please, calm yourselves children," the King said. "The kitten goes with you. Now let us take a bit of time to get to know your new friends, Belinda. I also have many things to discuss with your teacher before you are on your way. Take a few more cookies, a large helping of milk, and let's plan for your departure tomorrow morning. Will you need clothes and supplies?"

The talking, stories and questions continued into the evening. By nightfall the children were fast asleep and had to be carried off to bed.

Master Zhao, Godmother, and the royal family moved into the library, continuing to discuss the lessons the children needed how each would experience it.

"Master Zhao," the King began, "I have been a King for a very long time and I come from a long line of royalty." Master Zhao nodded. "There are a few basics that every good leader must learn. I just want to be sure somewhere in my granddaughter's adventures and lessons, she learns these basics."

The Prince added, "My lessons were extensive and interesting, but nothing like our Belinda will experience. However, I agree with Father, the basics are a must for one who will rule this kingdom."

"I have never heard you talk about this, my love," said Cinderella. "Whatever are you talking about—basics?"

Godmother smiled her most knowing smile and said, "The basics are—and correct me Master Zhao if I am wrong—four major areas one must know so well, they are recalled and used even under great duress: like fear, or in an emergency."

Master Zhao stood before Belinda's family. He seemed seven or even eight feet tall. He held out his hand and lifted his index finger. "One must have naturally or by practice, learned these valuable traits—number one: common-sense, number two: problem-solving, number three: wisdom, and number four: compassion." He fluttered his four long fingers as if he was playing piano keys. "These are the tools and treasures of any great leader."

The King, the Prince, Cinderella, and Godmother nodded in agreement. "That's it," cried the King. "Those are the four core traits every fine leader must learn or naturally have. Will you make sure these are sown into every lesson you teach these children, Master Zhao?"

"That I can promise," said the Teacher of All Teachers. "We will also cover all of the essentials—reading, writing, and math. Now, why don't you three retire? Godmother and I must continue to refine our plans."

Thank you so much, Master Zhao. We can rest easy for the first time in a long time," Cinderella said, stifling a yawn. "I'm sure I will sleep quite well tonight."

Satisfied the children would greatly benefit and enjoy the classroom experience, they said goodnight and went off to join the children in sleep.

Morning was announced by a noisy rooster. The servants had the children up and dressed and eating breakfast when Cinderella, the Prince, and King appeared just as the sun's rays began to peek over the blue-roofed towers of the castle.

A crowd gathered out in the courtyard where the wonderful classroom chairs were awaiting the children. Godmother was swinging her wand, eager to get going. Master Zhao stood beside the children preparing them for takeoff.

The King decided this event was worthy of a jubilant trumpet fanfare and signaled the royal trumpeters. The trumps sounded and the crowd became silent to listen to what the King would say.

He cleared his throat and spoke in his most powerful kingly voice: "Dear subjects, family, and honored guests—Godmother and Master Zhao. Today we are sending these three children to learn about the world, the laws of many lands, and about the tools of leadership. They will have an education like no other. Let us send them off with a mighty cheer and our heart's blessings. May they return to us soon." He cleared his throat again and continued. "My granddaughter, Belinda, has grown into a budding princess. We are very proud of her and the lessons she has learned thus far. She has shown courage in agreeing to continue her life lessons until she becomes a true princess. Bless your journey, children!"

The crowd echoed, "Bless you, children!"

Patsy Taking Off at the Palace

Patsy and Juan were already in their chairs. Belinda turned to take one last look at her family, her castle, and her subjects. "Goodbye, we will come back and visit now and again," she called to the crowd. "Mother, Daddy, Grandfather, I love you all. Don't worry about me. I have never been happier and I will learn how to be the best ruler I can be. And—" she could not hold back a giggle, "Melody and I, Juan and Patsy are going to have *so* much fun!"

Godmother and the teacher were already nearly three feet off the ground when Belinda's parents buckled her in for the ride, and hugged and kissed her goodbye. Then the wonderful chairs lifted off, zoomed twice overhead, and began to disappear. A thunder-like roar arose from the cheering crowd. The royal family waved until the children, their teacher, and Godmother were far away and out of sight. That evening, Cinderella, the Prince, and King returned to the library just before bedtime. Cinderella spoke first. "My heart is so happy, and I am not sure why, since my darling daughter has just left us again. Maybe it's because I know she is so fortunate and, my-oh-my, she will learn so much more than I did at her age!"

"I feel the same," said the Prince. "And, we truly can see her or have her visit if we think she needs us. Or," he winked at Cinderella, "if you become too lonely for her again."

"Well, children," said the King, "this has been quite a day. Belinda, our little Royal Princess is on her way to becoming a real princess. We are so proud of her. That teacher, Master Zhao, has been around for a long time and is quite knowledgeable. I am satisfied the children are in good hands."

"And Godmother is there, should we or the children need her," Cinderella said.

Godmother's laughter suddenly filled the room. She was nowhere in sight but they clearly heard her. "Remember, dear ones, Belinda will earn her royal crown as well as gain her second name. She has completed the first phase of her princess lessons. Sleep well."

The five travelers

The
End

Made in United States
Troutdale, OR
06/07/2024